**PANDA books are for young readers
making their own way
through books.**

D0104804

O'BRIEN SERIES FOR YOUNG READERS

 panda cubs

 pandas

 panda legends

flyers

Fireman Sinead!

ANNA DONOVAN
• pictures by Susan Cooper •

THE O'BRIEN PRESS
DUBLIN

First published 1997 by The O'Brien Press Ltd,
12 Terenure Road East, Rathgar, Dublin 6, Ireland.
Tel: +353 1 4923333; Fax: +353 1 4922777
E-mail: books@obrien.ie; Website: www.obrien.ie
Reprinted 1999, 2000, 2003, 2007, 2011, 2012.

ISBN: 978-0-86278-529-1

British Library Cataloguing-in-Publication Data
A catalogue record for this title is available from the British Library

7   8   9   10
12   13   14

Typesetting, layout, editing, design: The O'Brien Press Ltd
Printed and bound by CPI Group (UK) Ltd, Croydon, CR0 4YY
The paper in this book is produced using pulp from
managed forests.

The O'Brien Press receives assistance from

Can YOU spot the panda
hidden in the story?

'I want to be a fireman,'
said Sinead.
Dad looked a bit puzzled.
'I never heard of
a *girl* fireman!' he said.
Still, he made her
a special ladder
so she could practise.

Sinead climbed up and down
her ladder all day long.

'I'm going to be a fireman,'
she told her friend Tom.
'You can't!' he said.
'Only boys can be firemen.'

Sinead was not pleased.
'I can if I want,'
she said to Tom.
But she wasn't really sure.

'Mum!' she called. 'I'm going to be a fireman.'
'I never heard of
a *girl* fireman,' said Mum.
Still, she made a big, heavy,
floppy doll for Sinead
so she could practise.

Sinead called the doll Victim.
She carried him over her
shoulder. His long arms hung
down her back and his long
legs hung down her front.
Sinead was thrilled.

'Fireman Sinead to the rescue!'
she said to anyone who'd listen.

Tom laughed at her.
'You're silly,' he said.

But Sinead did not listen.
She practised on the ground.
Then she climbed the ladder,
slowly, holding Victim
carefully.

Finally, she put Victim
at her bedroom window –
and she rescued him!

Victim was rescued a hundred times a day. He was the most rescued doll ever.
But he didn't mind.
He just smiled and smiled, and hung over Sinead's shoulder, happy to be rescued again and again.

Then Sinead decided to do something more tricky.
Most fires happen at night, she thought. I must do some night practise.

At five o'clock in the morning
Sinead crept out of bed.
She put Victim at her window
ready to be rescued.
She got her ladder settled
against the wall.

Then she made a mistake ...

'Fire!' she screamed
at the top of her voice.

Dad leapt out of bed.
Mum came running.
Mrs Higgins next door
threw open her window,
shouting, 'Where? Where?'

Oh no! thought Sinead.

I'm in trouble!

And she was.

They all began to shout at her:

'You silly girl!'

'Go back to bed and
stop this noise!'

Only Victim smiled as he
leaned out the window
waiting to be rescued.
At least *he* didn't seem to mind.

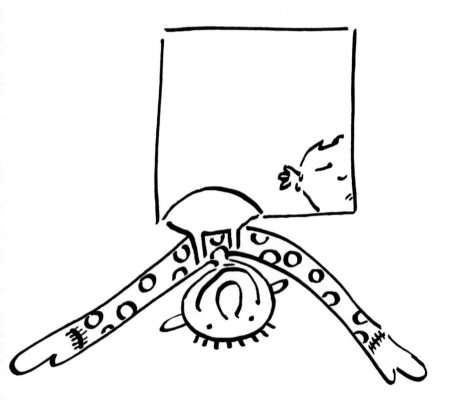

'I think Victim needs a rest,'
said Mum, calm at last.
'Come on, Sinead,
let's put him to bed.'

Mum and Sinead put Victim into Sinead's bed and tucked him up under the sheets.

'Now you can nurse him,'
said Mum.
'**Nurse?**' Sinead asked.
'Yes, NURSE!' said Mum firmly,
and off she went to her
own room.

Sinead looked at Victim,
who was still smiling.
'I don't think you *need* nursing!'
she said. 'You look
perfectly fine to me.'

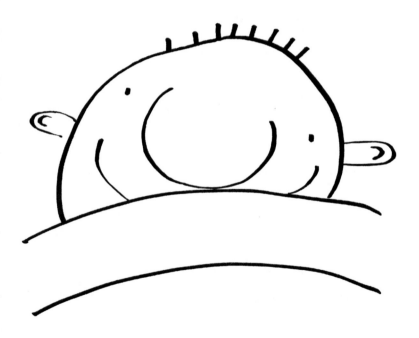

And she climbed into bed
beside him and dreamed about
being a fireman on a huge, red,
shiny engine, zooming down
the street to rescue someone.

A few days later there *was* a fire.
It was next door. Nobody knows
how it started. Someone said
Mr Higgins put a match
in the waste-paper bin.

The fire brigade came screaming down the road, lights flashing, siren going. Traffic got out of the way. People began to gather around the Higgins front gate.

Sinead came running
with her Mum.
'A real fire!' she said,
her eyes shining.

Tom came too with his Mum.
Sinead and Tom watched
every move of the firemen.
Sinead wanted to know
what else she should practise.

The men climbed quickly down
the ladders at the side of the
engine. One man unwound
a huge hose and another
looked for the water hydrant
on the street.

Others grabbed ladders
and ran to the house.
It all happened so fast
Sinead could hardly keep up.

One of the men noticed Sinead
watching closely and he
winked at her.
Sinead waved back.

Tom waved too.
'He's a real cool fireman,'
Tom said to Sinead.

The fire was not bad at all
and they had it out in no time.
Still, they went through
every room in the house
and turned the hose on
anything that was still hot.

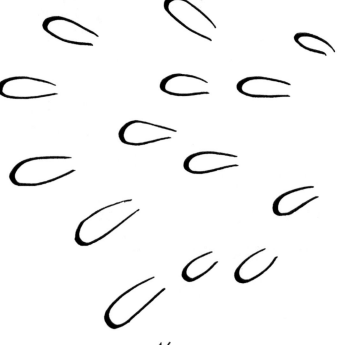

They left a bit of a mess
behind them.
Then they gathered their stuff
and began to reload the engine.

Sinead and Tom waved to
their fireman again.

The fireman pulled off his
helmet – and long curly hair
tumbled down his back.

Sinead looked more closely.
It WAS! It was a woman
fireman.

'Hey!' said Tom. 'That's not
a real fireman at all!'

But Sinead ran over to her.
'Mum and Dad and Tom said
there are no girl firemen!'
Sinead said.
'Ah, but they're wrong!' said the
fireman. 'Anyway, we're all
firefighters now. You want
to be one too, do you?'

Sinead could hardly say yes,
she was so pleased.
'I must practise a lot,' she said
to the firefighter.

The woman laughed.
'Good luck,' she said,
and she climbed up
on the huge engine.
The firefighters zoomed off
down the street.

Sinead turned to Mum.

'I'm going to be a firefighter!'
she said.

'Firefighter Sinead!' said Mum.

'It sounds okay to me.'

'I'm going to be a firefighter!'
Sinead said to Tom.
'Cool,' he said. 'And maybe
I'll be one too!'

'You must practise!' said
Sinead. 'But I can show you
everything.'

Well, did you find him?